PIA'S
PLANS

ALICE KUIPERS

ORCA BOOK PUBLISHERS

Published in Canada and the United States in 2020 by Orca Book Publishers.
orcabook.com

Library and Archives Canada Cataloguing in Publication
Title: Pia's plans / Alice Kuipers.
Names: Kuipers, Alice, 1979– author.
Series: Orca currents.
Description: Series statement: Orca currents
Identifiers: Canadiana (print) 2020017598x | Canadiana (ebook) 20200175998 | ISBN
9781459823785 (softcover) | ISBN 9781459823792 (PDF) |
ISBN 9781459823808 (EPUB)
Classification: LCC PS8621.U38 P53 2020 | DDC jc813/.6—dc23

Library of Congress Control Number: 2020930585

Summary: In this high-interest accessible novel for middle readers, Pia has been
desperately trying to make sure everything is perfect ever since her parents separated.

Orca Book Publishers is committed to reducing the consumption of
nonrenewable resources in the making of our books. We make
every effort to use materials that support a sustainable future.

Orca Book Publishers gratefully acknowledges the support for its publishing
programs provided by the following agencies: the Government of Canada,
the Canada Council for the Arts and the Province of British Columbia
through the BC Arts Council and the Book Publishing Tax Credit.

Edited by Tanya Trafford
Design by Ella Collier
Cover photograph by Gettyimages.ca/skynesher
Author photo by Emma Love

Printed and bound in Canada.

23 22 21 20 • 1 2 3 4

PIA'S PLANS

To Jackie. I am so thankful

for every writing minute.

Chapter One

I put my math workbook into my black bag. Dad bought it for me a year ago, but it looks brand-new. I clean it regularly. And I empty it as soon as I come home from school. I watched that show about tidying up. And how tidying up is magic. I think to myself, *Tidy bag, tidy mind.* I put two fingers on my wrist and count my heart rate. My heart seems to be beating normally.

Good. I slide my laptop into my bag and then close the silver clasp.

I call out to my sister, Nia. There's no answer. Weird. I wonder where she is. I text Jay to let him know that I'm on my way.

I grab a protein bar from Dad's pantry. I helped him organize things in here. Everything is labeled. All the dry goods are in glass jars. At least this space is tidy. The rest of his place is a complete mess. I glance over at the laundry basket. It's overflowing. I will run a load later tonight. My dirty running gear is in there. I am *not* going to think about the race earlier today. I check my heart rate again. My heart has sped up. Of course it has.

I go out the front door, closing it behind me. Outside it's warm. Fluffy, white clouds float in the sky. I check that I've locked the front door, then make my way to Jay's house. I put in my earbuds to listen to a short podcast—*Winning at Life*.

My phone rings. It's so loud that it hurts my eardrums.

"Hey, Pia, are you nearly here?" Jay asks.

"You know I am. I just told you I was on my way," I say into my cell phone. "Why are you being weird?" Jay and I have been best friends since we were four and in preschool.

"I'm not being weird," he says.

"Have you got everything ready? I don't want to waste any time."

"Everything's ready." He still sounds like he's being weird. He says, "I'm your best friend, aren't I? So, um, yeah. The books are out. Snacks are on the table."

I smile into my phone. "Perfect." We have a big math test every week for the next four weeks. I'm so stressed about it.

"But you've already studied loads for tomorrow," says Jay.

"Not enough. I really need tonight's study session. Thank you."

"Uh. Yeah."

"What? What's wrong?"

"Nothing. But how are you doing?" he asks.

"I'm okay." I sigh. I want to tell him that I'm not okay, not really. But saying it doesn't change what happened today. There's no point in telling him I feel terrible.

"I can't believe Panda B. won your race," he says.

Panda. That's really her name! She's the only Panda I know, but everyone calls her Panda B. Anyway, earlier today she won the Star track meet 400 meters. *My* race.

That's not the worst part. In the history of our school, the person who wins the Star track meet always wins the Aces track meet. It's destiny.

Except it's supposed to be *my* destiny to win. *Not* Panda's.

"I know," I say. "But, as they say, 'Aim to win next time.'" It's something I just heard on the podcast.

"Who says that? It seems intense."

"It is intense. But you do what you have to do. There's no way Panda B. is going to win the Aces race."

"I don't know, Pia. You know how it always goes. Panda B. won the Stars today. So maybe the next race…" He trails off.

I grit my teeth. "I'm never going to let her win again," I say.

"Okay, relax, Pia. You'll rock the math test tomorrow. But, um, well, maybe I should tell you something."

"You can tell me face-to-face," I say as I turn toward his house. "I'm here." I end the call.

Jay lives in a really cute house. It reminds me a bit of a box of chocolates. It has red wooden walls and white window trim. As I get closer I notice that the paint on the front door needs a touch-up. I should offer to help them get it all tidied.

Just as I knock I hear a strange noise coming from the backyard. Kind of a *shushing* sound. I frown.

Then I hear a *crash*, also from the backyard. Then giggles. I knock again. No one answers.

So, I walk around back. "Hello," I call as I go through the creaky gate. "Anyone here?"

And then it happens.

About ten people jump out of the bushes and from behind the old barbecue. "HAPPY BIRTHDAY!" everyone shouts. I see Nia with her friend Pippa. They're smiling and clapping. "We got you so good! You had no idea!"

I see Jay's mom. And several of our friends from school. I notice a table full of food. There are hot-dog buns, and there's a huge salad. "Happy birthday, Pia," Jay says. He jumps out at me from behind a garden chair.

"It's not my birthday," I say quietly.

"I know!" he cries. The excitement has clearly gotten to him. He's smiling so much! "I thought this could be your own special day. You never get that."

"We're supposed to study today," I say. My voice is trembling. I notice a cake. *Happy Birthday, Pia!* is scrawled across the top in loopy orange icing. Just my name on it. I've never had a cake with only my name on it before. It is a beautiful cake. White icing with little black musical notes all over it. Not many people know how much I love music.

I should feel happy.

But I don't even need to check to know that my heart rate is much higher than normal.

I lost the race today. It has basically been the worst day ever. Tomorrow was going to be better. I was going to study for the test and kick its butt.

This surprise party is a nightmare.

Of course, I know that I'm overreacting, but it feels like the worst thing that has ever happened to me. Worse even than coming in second to Panda B.

I can't be here. I have to leave.

I turn and march out of the yard.

"Where are you going?" I hear Nia yell.

Then Pippa's voice floats after me. "She's such a stress bomb."

I march down the street, away from the house. Away from the surprise party. I hear feet thundering along the sidewalk behind me.

"Pia! Wait up!" It's Jay.

I stop and take a slow breath. I notice that the sun is shining. The birds are singing. It could be a perfect evening. I glare at him. "You said we were going to study."

"Pia, I did this for you. You had a bad day."

"I didn't."

"You lost a race that was important to you."

"This race wasn't as important as the Aces. It was just...it was just a blip."

"A blip?"

"Like, it won't happen again. I just need to train harder. Work harder. And study for important things like math."

"What if you just took some time to relax? Would that be so bad? What if you let go of control and just enjoyed life once in a while?" Jay asks.

He doesn't understand. "The test tomorrow is important," I say.

"I know. But you do need to take a chill pill, Pia. I was trying to do something nice for you."

"Well, *don't!*" My voice comes out louder than I intended.

Even though he looks shocked, Jay says, "Come back to the party. You don't even have to say sorry."

"Sorry for what?" I yell again. "Just leave me alone!"

Jay's cheeks flush red. He stares at me for a long moment.

"I mean it," I say. "You don't understand how important all this is to me."

"No, I guess I don't," he says.

And then my best friend since forever turns around and walks away.

Chapter Two

One Week and One Day Later

I swallow back a yawn. I didn't sleep well. I was stressed about the math test. It is the second one. The first math test went well last week. Everything in my life would be perfect if I had won the Stars track meet. And if I had not had a fight with Jay.

I smooth my bed and tuck in my sheet. I straighten the picture over my bed. It reads, *A Goal Without a Plan Is Just a Wish*. I double-check that my black school bag is packed. Then I pull my tidy bobbed hair into a short ponytail. I'm ready for my workout. I pull out my phone and check the list I made last night when I was having trouble falling asleep:

Goals Today

Listen to podcast *Being Your Best Self*

Warm up, then work out

Two rounds:

50 push-ups

50 sit-ups

50 squats

Drink eight glasses of water

Eat five fruits and veggies

Excel in math test, third period

Win 400-meter gold at Aces track meet!

Thought for the day: "The work of today is the history of tomorrow, and we are its makers." —Juliette Gordon Low.

I have a book of inspirational quotes that I keep by my bed for a little nighttime reading.

I read this quotation a few times. It means that if I work hard today, I'm making history. I imagine myself making history. Well, maybe not making history in the world. But at least making history in my school.

Sure, Panda B. won the last race. And as Jay so kindly reminded me, whoever wins the Stars always wins the Aces.

But not today.

I am going to win today. It's all about visualization. I imagine myself accepting the gold medal. If I can see it, I can make it happen. When I win this track meet, I'll be the best at school at everything. Best in all my subjects and best at track. Then, hopefully, it won't matter so much that my best friend isn't talking to me.

I sigh. I bite my bottom lip, but when I notice myself doing it, I stop. It's a bad habit. I look over my list and sigh when I get to the part about the fruits and vegetables. I like strawberries and bananas just fine, and broccoli isn't the worst. But eating five fruits and veggies a day seems impossible. I always get to four and then start stressing about number five.

But I will keep trying. I will *strive*. I love that word. It makes me feel like I'm doing well even when I say it.

"Strive," I say out loud.

I look over at my alarm clock. Oh no. It's already six thirty! I haven't listened to my podcast or done my workout. I decide to do both together. About thirty minutes later I'm all sweaty and I can't remember anything they said on the podcast. I check my heart rate. Racing. I take some deep breaths, trying not to panic.

Now all I need to do is shower and have a healthy breakfast. And I already have that covered. Dad and I made buckwheat muffins with blueberries last night. Perfect.

I love the word *perfect*. *Perfect*. That's the word Mom says all the time. *Perfect*. And I love trying to make her say it. She always looks so happy when she does. *Perfect*.

I step out of my room, heading for the shower.

My heart rate speeds up immediately. Loud music is booming from the room down the hall. There is stuff everywhere.

My sister. Also known as the biggest hurdle to my life being calm and perfect.

Her clothes are all over the banisters. Her schoolbooks are on the floor. I can hear her singing loudly in the shower. There is a wet towel on the floor outside the bathroom door. How did she get a towel wet before she even got into the shower?

"Nia!" I call, banging on the door.

Nia and Pia. Yep. Those are our names. I have no idea what our parents were thinking. Dad says our names are cute. Mom says they are perfect.

Argh.

"Nia?" I call again. "Are you going to be long?"

She keeps singing that annoying pop song. And it's not even the same one blasting out of her room. I follow the trail of clothes down the hall. There are more strewn all over her bedroom floor. Magazines and dance stuff are everywhere too. She is obsessed with everything to do with dance. Her favorite styles are acro and contemporary. Over her bed she has a picture of a dancer flying through the air. At the bottom of the poster it reads, *Dare to Dream*.

I check my phone. How long is she going to take? We have to get to school. I head back to the bathroom.

"Nia, get out of the shower. NOW!" I yell.

"Can't make me! I'm washing my hair." So she can hear me.

"We're going to be late for school. I'm setting my timer. In four minutes you'd better be out of there, or I'm going to kill you."

At four minutes my phone pings.

Nothing happens. If anything, Nia starts singing more loudly. I bang on the door. None of this is working, I tell myself. I try to stay calm. I step back from the door and wait. I take five deep breaths. I do feel calmer.

Finally, Nia flounces out of the bathroom, wrapped in a towel. I'm about to say thank you when I notice something.

It's my towel.

I glance at her wet towel on the floor. Now it makes sense.

"That's my towel," I say to her. My voice is dangerously quiet.

Suddenly I lunge.

I try to yank the towel off her, but I step on one of her books that's lying at the top of the curved, carpeted staircase.

I slip.

What happens next is like a stupid cartoon for little kids. My hands grab at thin air.

I don't have hold of the towel. Or anything.

"Help!" I scream.

Nia steps forward to try to grab me, but it's too late—I'm already falling.

I fall down the stairs in a mad cartwheel.

I land on my ankle and then crumple in a heap.

Pain shoots from my foot all the way up to my brain.

"Nia!" I scream. "I think I broke my leg!"

Chapter Three

Annoying as my sister is, she gets down the stairs very fast.

"Oh my god! Are you okay?"

"I don't know! Help me up. Ow, ow, ow!" I yell as she lifts me to standing.

"What should we do? Should I call Dad?" she asks. She's holding her towel around herself. Dad has already gone to work.

"I have to think. I need to sit down."

She helps me hobble into the living room and onto the sofa. Somehow, she does it without dropping her towel.

"Pia, what do we do?" she asks.

"It's okay. It's not as bad as I thought," I say. I keep my voice calm even though my ankle is killing me. I know that if we call our parents, they will freak out, and my plans for the day will be ruined.

Nia starts to cry. "I'm sorry my book was on the floor. It's all my fault."

"It's okay. It's no big deal."

"But what about your track meet today? How can you race? Look how swollen your ankle is already."

I take a big breath. I imagine I am blowing out a candle. I heard this in a podcast about staying calm. I focus on being in the moment. I look around the living room. Dad's stuff is everywhere. It looks like someone has robbed us, although I know they haven't. His house is always like this. From where I'm sitting I can see into the kitchen. The remains of his breakfast are all over the counters. How can one person make so much mess? Mom's house is always so clean and tidy. Dad is pure chaos. Nia is just like him, and I am just like Mom.

Sometimes I wish I didn't have to be like Mom. Like right now, while Nia is crying. And my ankle is hurting so much.

"Get my phone," I order. "And get dressed. I'm fine. We have to get to school."

She does as I tell her. Normally she would fight me. But I guess my red, puffy ankle makes her obey.

I rotate my foot with both hands.

Ouch. "Get me some clothes too!" I shout. "Please," I add. I'm sweaty and gross, but I can't get up the stairs to have a shower. My ankle will feel better in a minute, I'm sure.

But I keep thinking, The track meet. The track meet.

There's no way something like a sore ankle is going to stop my plans for the day. I tell Nia to get me a bandage from the upstairs bathroom. I know exactly where the bandages are and how to put one on. I bought Dad a first-aid kit as a moving-in gift.

Nia and I hobble to the bus stop. Halfway there she stops. "Pia, I forgot my backpack!"

I stare at her like she's an alien. How could she forget it? How could I not have noticed?

I even turn her around to make sure her backpack isn't somehow, magically, on her back.

It's not.

"Nia! What were you thinking? What about your lunch and your form for your trip? It has to be in today! Mom told me to make sure you took it."

She bursts into tears again.

She looks a bit like a pug, my favorite type of puppy. They have squished-in faces and always seem like they are crying. Nia's brown eyes are round and sad. I give her a hug.

"It's okay. Run back fast and get it. I think we've got time." I am remembering that when she brought clothes downstairs for me just now, she included my super-lucky shirt. Mom bought it for me for getting the highest score in language arts. It has a blue guitar on it, and it is made of soft material. Every time I wear it, something good happens. Today will be fine.

Nia races back. I stand on the sidewalk, waiting. I think about how Dad's house still feels like his house. Not mine. It's been two years and six months since we began spending half our time living there. Mom's house doesn't feel like home either. They sold our house when they got divorced. Some other perfect family lives there now.

I breathe out slowly. I listened to a podcast on this. When my thoughts are racing, I'm feeling anxious. I tell myself to calm down. There's nothing to be anxious about.

And then the school bus goes by.

My anxiety goes through the top of my head. It feels like that anyway. It feels like I'm exploding with stress.

"Nia!" I scream to the empty sidewalk. I turn to walk back toward the house. Then I decide to try to race to the bus instead. It's a block away and pulling up to our stop.

"Coming!" she yells. She appears at our doorway. At least she has her backpack now.

"Run!" I yell. Then I start to run.

Well, I try to run. But my ankle hurts too much. If my ankle could scream, it would be screaming, *STOP RUNNING!* But ankles can't scream. They're ankles.

My mind is full of racing thoughts.

The bus is at our stop.

Pure panic fills my brain.

I cannot miss the bus.

I cannot hurt my ankle more.

Nia races past me. She might make it. Then the bus will wait for me. It's going to be okay!

"Run, Nia!" I yell at her.

She turns back, a look of shock on her face. I guess that's because for once she's running faster than me.

Because she turns back, she stops running.

Because she stops running, the bus leaves our stop.

The bus is gone.

I can't believe it!

Now what are we going to do?

We cannot be late for school.

I will die.

Nia comes over to me. "Are you okay, big sister?"

It's a running joke between us. Even though we're twins, identical twins, she calls me big sister. I call her little sister. I'm only five minutes older than her, but still. And we couldn't be more different in personality. I'm much, much, much more mature than she is. She's all bad grades and lost homework and giggling in class.

"I'm okay."

"You're not," she says. "You're totally drama."

That's something else she always says to me. *Totally drama*. It's not a real saying, but in our family it gets said all the time. Apparently it started when I was five. I said it when I was upset because the page where I had drawn letter M was missing from my preschool alphabet book. It had got lost.

Or something.

I don't want to think about it.

"I'm not totally drama."

"So you're not thinking you're going to die?" Nia puts her hand on her hip. She looks a lot like Mom when she does that. Which is weird. Because I'm the twin like Mom.

"Of course I don't think I'm going to die."

"Then why do you look like a volcano about to explode?"

"Shut up," I say. "If anyone's totally drama, it's you."

"I missed my bus for you," she says.

"Are you kidding me right now?" I yell.

A car pulls up behind her.

Oh my god, I think. We're about to be abducted!

The window rolls down.

"Don't look," I say to Nia. "Stranger danger."

She bursts out laughing. "That's Beck and his dad, goofball."

Oh. "Don't call me that," I say. I look over at the car. She's right. It's Beck. The quietest boy in our class. He's always the last to arrive and the first to leave. He doesn't really talk to or interact with anyone in class— he always looks like he would rather be alone. His dad is the opposite—he's on all the school committees and involved with every aspect of school life. He's also very involved with the community and the city. And, oddly enough, he is also good friends with our dad. They're both divorced, and they hang out together. They talk about being divorced and stuff. Not that they know Nia and I listen at the top of the stairs.

"Hey, girls," Mr. Lopez calls. "I saw you miss your bus. Come on. We can give you a ride. I'll text your dad and let him know."

Beck is leaning his head back on the passenger seat. He has his eyes closed, like he's trying to pretend none of this is happening. He never comes over to our house with his dad.

Nia is already dragging me toward the car. We scramble into the back seat. "Thanks, Mr. Lopez."

"No problem. You girls are in class with Beck this year, right? Why don't you ever invite them over?" He pokes Beck in the ribs playfully. Then he begins to drive.

Beck doesn't speak. Instead he reaches forward and turns on the stereo. He taps on his phone, and a song starts. I recognize it right away. It's by Bombargo. I know this because:

1. They are my favorite band in the world.
2. I listen to this song all the time. It's one of their best.

I've never met anyone else who knows their music. Except for Jay. But I don't want to think about Jay.

Before I realize I'm speaking out loud, I say, "I love this band."

Beck says, "Really? You know who they are?"

"Sure."

"She knows everything about music, Beck," Nia adds.

"Do you really?" he says, looking at me.

I shrug.

"You've never talked about music at school," he says. He sounds like he's accusing me of a crime.

"Not to you," I snap.

Beck's dad laughs. "Oh ho! This one's a firecracker!" he says.

We spend the rest of the car ride in awkward silence. I try to think of something polite to say, but I can't. And I'm annoyed at being called a firecracker. What even is that? I look out the window and feel a strong satisfaction when we pass the school bus.

We get to school a full fifteen minutes earlier than we would normally. I think for a second about how

Beck is always last to class. If he gets to school before everyone else, what does he do before class every day?

I'm glad we're here early. Maybe today isn't going to be so bad after all.

My ankle screams as I get out of the car. Not that ankles can scream. But, yet again, it feels like it's screaming.

Maybe today is going to be even worse than I thought.

Chapter Four

"So, Bombargo?" Beck asks as we walk toward school. Well, he walks. I hobble.

Nia races off to chat with her crowd. She's always in a crowd.

"You're early!" Pippa screams as soon as she spots her. Pippa is always so loud!

"I love them," I say. "My favorite song is 'Tangerine High,' although 'Oxygen' is also super good."

"Do you know they're from Saskatoon?"

"Of course I do." I realize we're walking away from the classroom, toward the library. "Where are we going?" I ask.

"Oh, you don't have to come. I just always hang in the library before class. I don't want to do the small-talk thing."

"What's the small-talk thing?"

"You know, how everyone just talks about nothing?"

"Sure," I say. "I get it." And I completely do. Nia is amazing at small talk. I've always found it really hard to think of things to say to people on the spot. "What do you do in the library?"

He pulls out his phone and opens up an app. "Mostly I'm on this," he says. He tilts the screen, and I see multiple guitar chords. "It breaks down the music for all kinds of cool songs." We stand in the hallway and search out a bunch of songs we both love. Neither of us really notices the crush of kids coming in as the bell rings. When I look up we're in the middle of the kids flowing past, like two rocks in a river. I imagine us as rocks in a river anyway.

"I write song lyrics," I blurt—then immediately wish I hadn't said anything.

Beck looks at me. "Cool."

"Well, I try to write them. But then I get stuck. I want the song to be perfect, and I worry it's no good." Oh, why can't I stop talking? Beck is just so easy to talk to.

"You can always rewrite it after," he says. He pauses. "You don't seem like a songwriter."

"What do you mean?"

"Well, you're always just so organized and, you know, top of the class."

"That has nothing to do with writing songs. I just work hard to do well at school," I snap. "I don't get why people think that's so weird."

"Who says it's weird?" he asks.

"My sister. My ex-best friend."

"You mean Jay?"

I shrug.

"What happened with you two?" Beck asks. "I noticed you weren't hanging out lately."

"We got into a fight. It was nothing." I look around the empty hallway. Panic rises in me. Like floodwater rising. That's how it feels to me. "Where is everyone?"

"In class," Beck says. He frowns. I notice only one of his eyebrows is lowered, though, giving him a funny, lopsided look. Or it would be funny if I wasn't feeling so stressed.

"In class!" I shriek. I am as loud as Pippa. So. Loud!

"It's not a big deal," says Beck.

"I have to go."

We hobble toward the class. Well, I hobble. Beck walks slowly beside me. He is clearly not worried about being late.

"Are you still planning to do the track meet today?" he asks.

"Oh yes. Nothing is going to get in the way of my plan."

"Your plan?"

"I have to win. There's no other option." I say it firmly. I even think my ankle feels better as I say it.

Mr. Wolfe pauses as we walk into class. "Ah, nice of you to join us."

Beck taps his eyebrow with a finger and then waves his hand. It's more like a half wave.

Mr. Wolfe says, "Lateness is not tolerated in this class, Beck. And Pia, I expect better of you."

"Of course." I want to say sorry, but I can't. The word *sorry* makes me feel like puking. I've always had trouble with it. I think because it means I'm admitting I've made a mistake. My heart beats faster, and I sit quickly. I blow out a pretend candle to calm down.

"Did you study?" Beck whispers.

"Of course I did!" I say. And then I realize he's sitting next to me. What, are we friends now? I look up and see Jay at the desk in front of me. His shoulders are stiff and tense. My best friend ever, and he still won't speak to me. I square my jaw. It's not my fault. He's wrong and that's all there is to it. If he can't see that he's wrong, then that's his problem. I'll show him today when I win the track meet. Organization and perfection. That's how you manage. Not stupid surprise parties or anything like that.

Mr. Wolfe says something as he passes out the math test. Oh no. I must have heard him wrong.

"Did he just say exponents?" I ask Beck urgently.

"Sure. That's the test today."

"But I studied linear functions!" My voice is much louder than I intended it to be. At least half the class turns to look at me. Not Jay, I notice.

Pippa says, "Ooooh, Pia, what are you going to do? You studied for the wrong test! You made a mistake! Does that mean you're normal like the rest of us?"

The whole class starts laughing.

Even Nia laughs. My own sister. "It's not funny, Nia," I say loudly. I realize that two people aren't laughing. Beck and Jay.

"It is kind of funny, Pia," says Nia. "For you of all people." But I think she realizes I'm about to start crying because she adds, "Oh, I'm sorry, big sis. It's just not like you to make a mistake. That's all Pippa was saying."

"Calm down, everyone, please," says Mr. Wolfe. "Pia, you'll just have to do your best."

"My *best*? But what if it's not good enough?" I stammer.

"Settle down, everyone. Pia, you'll be fine. Sit down."

I guess at some point I had stood up. My ankle throbs. I sit down and turn over the test. I feel like I am drowning in a sea of words and numbers I don't understand. I know I'm not really drowning, but that's what it feels like. Because I know I'm going to fail this test.

Chapter Five

By recess my mood is a mixture of anxiety and despair.
And because my ankle is hurting, I am the last kid to
get to the vending machine for my drink.

I always drink white milk. Every day. It's healthy
and I love it. But our school vending machine never
has many white milks. Because I'm the last one to
recess today, the vending machine is out of white milk.

I never, ever miss the white milk.

I buy chocolate milk, and as I stand there trying to open it, I start to wobble.

I guess my ankle is hurt worse than I thought. I lose my balance and spill chocolate milk all over myself.

All over my lucky shirt. Now the blue guitar is a sticky brown. And the kids who are standing around the vending machine are laughing.

Everyone is laughing at me. That's twice in one morning!

It's my worst nightmare.

I head to the washroom and try to clean my shirt.

It doesn't help. The stain is going to be there forever.

My favorite shirt is destroyed.

This is the worst day I've ever had.

I make a list of everything that has gone wrong.

1. Hurt my ankle

2. Missed the bus

3. Studied for the wrong math test

4. Ruined my favorite shirt

What's happening? This day is a disaster.

I look in the bathroom mirror. I admit, as I look at my face, that the biggest of all my problems is the fight I had with Jay.

It was bad last week when I lost that race. But at least I had my friend. Oh, why did he have to throw that stupid party for me? He ruined everything.

I sit. On the bathroom floor. Super gross. But I can't stand up anymore.

I pull out my phone.

I want to write down my feelings. I love to write song lyrics. This is a big secret. Normally. Except today I told Beck. What is wrong with me?

I remember what you said to me
The way it made me feel
The way I need to be
In control

Got to hold on tightly

Got to hold on tightly

Pippa and Nia come in.

"YUCK!" Nia cries. "You can't sit on the floor!"

"You're right," I say.

This surprises both of us.

I put my phone away quickly. What am I even doing on the floor? Even Nia doesn't know that I love to *write* songs. I try to get to my feet, and she pulls up.

"How are you doing?" she asks.

"Great," I say. I put on a huge smile.

Pippa snorts and laughs. Most days, I hate Pippa. I *really* hate her right now.

"You can't do the track meet," Nia says.

"I'm fine. It'll be fine. I *have* to win it, Nia."

"You can't even stand up properly." Suddenly she yawns. And then rubs her eye.

Oh no. I know what that means.

"Nia!" I say. "Are you okay?" I'm worried she's about to get a migraine. She has been getting them since she was four.

I expect her to say she's fine, like she usually does. But she looks at me for a long moment. Then it is her turn to surprise me.

"I think I'm getting a migraine," she says.

It's the first time she's ever said this. Normally she tries to ignore the signs that a migraine is coming on. She pretends there's nothing wrong. She ends up sick for days. It drives me crazy! Because sometimes, if she takes her meds quickly, her migraines only last about two hours. If Mom or I notice the migraine starting, we insist Nia take her meds. We are always paying attention to see if a migraine has started. And Nia always fights us about her medication.

"You need to take your medication and get home," I say.

"I know!" she snaps.

Even though she's snappy, I'm delighted, and shocked, that she's agreeing with me.

We head to the office. Ms. Jensen hands over Nia's medication once we've explained what's going on. I've already called Mom. Nia sits in a corner, her hands over her eyes. Bright lights make the headaches worse. Migraines are horrible. Most people don't realize that kids can get migraines. But our doctor told us that one in ten kids suffers from them. When Nia gets a migraine, she often barfs. When she was little, she used to barf a lot.

The bell rings. The hallways fill up with kids. It's very noisy. I hope Mom gets here soon.

She arrives pretty quickly. "Hey, bear," she says to me. She sits down next to Nia, who is very quiet and serious-looking. "Shall we get you home, monkey?" she says to her.

Mom asks me how my day's going before she and Nia leave, but I can tell she's worried about Nia, so I don't fill her in on everything that's happened today.

We all hate Nia's migraines. They come regularly, and Mom always stresses about them.

So do I.

"Everything's tip-top perfect," I say. "Nia was happy to take her meds because she knew a migraine was starting."

Mom's eyes widen. "You're a star," she says to Nia. "And so are you," she says to me. "Thanks for looking after your little sister." She smiles. I love it when she smiles.

"Love you," she calls as they leave. I don't say it back, but I wave. It occurs to me that I haven't spent much time with Mom or Nia recently. I mean, I see my sister every day, but I haven't properly talked to her lately. I've been so busy with track and studying. And when was the last time I did something fun with Mom? Going between Mom's house and Dad's house, I always feel like I never have time to just sit and hang out. Maybe we should all watch a movie tonight, after the meet. We could make popcorn. Like we used to.

But I forgot. I have to study tonight. The math test today was a disaster. I know I'll have to retake it tomorrow. I have to study. There's no time to hang out with Mom or Nia.

I sigh. At least my ankle is feeling better. Well, kind of better. I hobble to class. I'm going to make this day turn around. It's going to be a great day. It's all up to me.

Chapter Six

My language arts class is great. This day really is turning around! We are doing a poetry unit, and I spend some time researching songs and poems. We are learning about how songwriting and poetry are linked. I learn that musical artists sometimes publish their song lyrics as poetry. I drift into a fantasy where I publish my own book one day—full of song lyrics and poetry.

And then I spend the rest of the class writing. Composing. That's what Ms. Steele calls it. Composing! It is a great word to describe what I'm doing. I feel like I disappear into the words. Of course, I don't really disappear into the words, but it seems like I do. It's as if the words are all that matter. And it's amazing. When I'm composing I don't feel stressed. I'm not worrying about my grades or about being the best.

Suddenly Ms. Steele says, "Thank you, everyone, for your hard work today." The class went by so quickly that I hardly noticed the time. Ms. Steele stops by my desk as I'm packing up my things. "Pia, you were very focused on the assignment today," she says. "You weren't checking your heart rate or looking quite so worried."

"Checking my heart rate?" I ask. I thought that was one of my secrets! I check my pulse several times a day. I worry that my heart is beating too fast.

"I've noticed you putting your fingers to your wrist. I recognized what you were doing because I used to do the same thing." She leans against a desk. "You know, a lot of kids are very anxious and worried. Life is stressful."

I swallow hard.

"We have a school counselor here. Mrs. Amore. Did you know that? You can come and talk about anything, if you're feeling worried."

"I don't have anything to worry about," I say. Which, of course, is absolutely not true.

"Everyone has stuff they worry about," says Ms. Steele with a small smile. "It's normal. You can't control your thoughts. But you can control how you react to those thoughts."

"I feel worried about my grades," I blurt out. "What if I don't do well at school? And I feel like I have to look after Nia all the time. We go between Mom's house and Dad's house, but Nia's always losing stuff. I feel like I have to be the grown-up."

"That's a lot to worry about, Pia."

"If I don't do well at school, then I'll never be able

47

to look after Nia when we are actual adults. I won't ever get a good job! And I had a big fight with Jay last week." Tears spring to my eyes.

"I noticed you two weren't sitting next to each other."

"Well, he had a surprise party for me."

She looks puzzled. "That's nice."

"It was, but he *knows* I like everything to be planned. He knows I like to be in control. He should have known I wouldn't want anything like that."

"I see," Ms. Steele says.

"Without telling me, he invited a few of our friends and Nia over. And he put together a barbecue with his mom. I told him once that I'd never had a birthday without Nia. So he made the party just for me. Not Nia. But it wasn't even my birthday! It was a random date. I didn't expect it. He told me to come over to study for a test. Then I got there, and everyone jumped out and yelled, 'HAPPY BIRTHDAY!'"

"Sounds like he was trying to do something lovely for his friend."

"Maybe, but I felt like I was going to die. I was in full panic mode and stressed about the test." I look down at my shoes. But the words keep coming. "So I left. He came after me and asked me why I was so upset. And I told him and now we're not speaking." Much to my embarrassment, I feel a tear trickle down my cheek. I am so glad everyone else has left the classroom.

Ms. Steele says, "Pia, what if you didn't feel responsible for Nia?"

I laugh. "That's never going to happen."

"What if you tell Jay you're sorry?"

"But I'm *not* sorry. It was his fault. He should never have told me we were going to be studying. He knew that test was important."

Ms. Steele folds her arms and says gently, "Tests are important, Pia. You're right. But as you get older, you have to be able to strive for balance."

Strive. I love that word. "I don't strive for balance," I say. "I strive to be the best."

"None of us are the best. We're each just ourselves."

The whole conversation is making me more and more stressed. I feel my breathing speed up. "I have to go," I say.

"Pia, wait."

"Really, I have to go." I hurry out of the classroom and head to the lunchroom.

I try to shake off the conversation. But the words *strive for balance* keep playing in my head. What does that even mean?

I get to the cafeteria late. My ankle is still hurting, but not as badly as it was earlier. We have hundreds of kids at our school, so the lunchroom is huge. It's so loud it feels like every single one of them is already here.

Cafeteria chaos.

I choose chicken fingers and fries. I add broccoli. It'll be one of the five fruits and vegetables for the day. I forgot to eat my blueberry muffin this morning.

When I pick up my tray, my ankle buckles. Worse than when I wobbled with the chocolate milk. I can't stay standing! As I struggle to regain my balance, the tray slips from my hands and flips. The broccoli, chicken fingers and fries fly.

As I fall to the floor, I watch with horror as a piece of broccoli lands in Pippa's hair.

She screams. And then everything goes crazy!

Chapter Seven

Pippa yells, "Who threw that?" She doesn't see me on the floor. Instead she looks over at three boys in the grade ahead of us. "For real?" she screams. "You want to get my attention, just ask me! Don't you *dare* throw stuff at me!"

Pippa is very annoying. But she has some great qualities. Her best quality is that she speaks her mind. She stands up for women and girls and doesn't tolerate bullies. She's a warrior princess. And right now, before I have time to get to my feet and tell her that the broccoli is mine, she's standing up. For women. For girls. And for herself. Or at least she thinks she is.

She grabs a chicken finger and flings it.

It lands on one of the boys. "What?" the boy yells. "I didn't do anything!"

But Pippa is on a mission. She throws another chicken finger at the same boy.

"Stop picking on me!" he cries.

"*Picking* on you?" Pippa exclaims. "Did you hear that?" She turns to the room like she's at a political rally. She raises both her palms to the ceiling. "You threw broccoli at *me*! Do you expect me to just stand here and take it?" Then she grabs a third chicken finger. She hurls it at him.

He ducks and scoops a handful of fries. He throws them in her general direction. "I didn't throw anything at you!"

The fries scatter.

There are now fries on at least six kids, as well as on people's food trays. A fry covered in ketchup lands on the shirt of a girl sitting next to Pippa.

"That's it. You asked for it!" Pippa screams.

She stomps over and dumps her chocolate milk on the head of one of the other boys.

"Food fight!" someone yells. The other kids who have fries on them are laughing. They start throwing food too.

Fries. Chicken fingers. Broccoli. Lettuce. Sausages. Ketchup.

Kids are yelling. Some with anger. Some with joy. Some with both. The cafeteria is a mix of crazed rage and joyful silliness. It's almost beautiful to watch. Until someone nearly stands on my head. I haul myself up.

Mr. Walker jumps onto a table. I realize he's been yelling at us all for about five minutes.

I realize that I'm standing.

And that I have someone else's chicken finger in my hand. I caught it.

Problem is, I am about to throw it back.

My arm is already pulled back. I realize what's happening as my arm releases. I can't stop it. Not my arm. And not the chicken finger.

It flies through the air.

It hits Mr. Walker right in the chest.

The effect is like the room has been electrocuted.

Of course, the room hasn't been electrocuted.

But it feels like it has. Because everyone is shocked into silence.

The original piece of broccoli falls out of Pippa's hair.

I notice that.

I notice Mr. Walker turn to me.

He sees my hand, which is open.

"Pia!" he yells, shocked. "You started this?"

"I didn't start it. It was an accident. I fell—"

"Do not talk back to me. Did you or did you not just throw a chicken finger at me?"

My mouth opens. But no words come out.

How has this happened?

I see Jay staring at me. There is sympathy in his gaze.

And it makes me furious.

I don't want his sympathy. I don't need anyone's help. I'm in control.

Mr. Walker yells, "Pia, I'm talking to you!"

I try again to speak.

The words won't come out. I want to say, *There's an explanation. I fell. It's a misunderstanding.*

But no words come.

I imagine that I look like a fish in water, my mouth opening and closing.

This thought does not help. It just makes me more embarrassed.

Which makes Jay look even more sympathetic.

Which makes me *more* angry.

"This is the worst day of my life!" I yell.

Looking like a fish was bad. Yelling at a teacher is much, much worse.

I could not have made Mr. Walker more angry. "Don't yell at me!" he yells.

"But you're yelling at me!" I reply.

Pippa turns and looks at me with frank astonishment. "Go, girl!" she cries. It's a warrior-princess cry.

It does not help.

I didn't mean to talk back to Mr. Walker.

He has turned a strange shade of red. Almost a purple red. "What do you have to say for yourself, Pia?" Mr. Walker sputters.

My mouth is back to being a fish mouth.

"Detention, Pia," he says calmly. "Now, everyone, clean up this mess and start acting like you're in the upper grades. That is more than enough."

Did he say detention?

Detention?

I've never had a detention. Does that go on my school record? What if I never get into college? What if I never get a good job? All because of this detention!

My life is truly over now.

"Pia, you'll serve your detention after the track meet. Our school is counting on our team to do well today. Maybe you can make up for this mess! Although, I know that Panda B. won last week."

Mentioning Panda B. makes everything worse! I want to say, *My ankle is killing me. I can't even stand up without falling over and causing a massive food fight.* But I don't speak. All I can think is that I have to race.

Because I have to win.

I have to make this day better. I need to show everyone, especially Jay, that I'm okay. Better than okay. I have to show them that I'm the best.

Chapter Eight

I limp to the bus that will take us to the track meet. I keep thinking about my detention. I will have to tell Mom that I need to go back to school for detention. She'll be watching the track meet. I don't know how to tell her.

As I get to the bus, I make a decision. I'm not going to get on the bus. I will avoid Mom and the race. It's is a perfect way out of this mess. My brain hurts too much to face Mom. My ankle hurts too much to race.

I look for Miss Singhal to tell her I'm not coming.

But when she sees me, she beams. "Here's our superstar!"

It makes me feel good. It makes me feel better than good. It makes me feel amazing. It helps me forget my disastrous day. It makes me feel like I can do anything.

I get on the bus. A superstar. That's what I am.

My mind is a tornado. Of course, it's not a tornado, but it feels like it's spinning around and around. One minute I feel out of control. The next minute, everything is fine. It's so confusing!

I flop into a seat by myself. I don't want to sit next to anyone.

Especially not Jay, who is getting on the bus. What is he even doing here? He's not on the team. He looks at the empty space beside me. I move my bag to cover the seat. Jay looks sad as he walks past. I hear him sit down right behind me. Argh. Worse, Panda B. gets on the bus and waves at me. "Hi, Pia! I bet you're looking forward to losing this race."

"I'm not going to lose," I say.

"I won the Stars. Right? I'm going to win the Aces. It's how things always go."

"Not today," I say.

"Sure. If you say so. But remember, I won the Stars. If you were the best, how could that even happen?"

I can't answer her.

Beck moves my bag and flops into the seat next to me.

"Why are you here?" I say shortly.

"Hi, Pia. Nice to see you too," Beck says. "You don't need to be so moody."

I sigh. "Hi, Beck. I'm just surprised, that's all."

"I'm reporting for the school newsletter."

"Really?"

The bus rumbles away from the school. The energy inside is happy and excited. If my ankle weren't so sore, and if my day had been going better, I'd be happy and excited too.

Maybe.

Or maybe I'd be stressed and worried like I usually am.

I check my heart rate, lightly holding my fingers to my wrist and counting. My pulse is normal. But my heart feels like it's racing.

"Hello, Earth to Pia," Beck says. "Are you listening?"

"What? I was just...um...could you say that again?"

Jay leans forward. "She won't say sorry."

"Jay!" I say.

"Just telling your new friend so he doesn't expect it."

"Okay, man," Beck says to Jay.

"She just hates the word *sorry*."

"Well," Beck says, "maybe I'm okay with that." He turns to me, ignoring Jay, who slumps back into his seat. I feel relieved that Jay isn't talking to us anymore.

"The newsletter wants an interview," Beck says. "Maybe we can interview you?"

"*Me?*"

"Sure. School hero! Top grades. Great runner. We want to hear what you have to say."

"But what if I say something stupid?"

"Then we can edit it."

"Edit it? Isn't that cheating?"

"No, that's writing. I'll record you and then check it later to make sure it all makes sense. If you say something that doesn't make sense, I'll cut it out. Most of writing is rewriting."

"Huh. So what sort of writing do you do?"

"This. Nonfiction. I don't like making stuff up. I like reporting on what's real. Interviews and news stories. I want to be a reporter maybe. Or run my own online news source. That and play in a band, of course."

"Are you in a band?"

"I was. But two of the other guys moved away—they were brothers. And so I'm looking for two new band members. I have one guy. He goes to a different school. He's awesome. Bass guitar. So I need a drummer and a lead singer."

"A lead singer?"

Jay leans forward. "Pia has a great voice."

"Would you just shut up, Jay?" I snap. "First you're mean, and now you're oversharing. Why are you even on this bus? You're not on the team." Not that it matters what he said. I'm not going to sing in Beck's band. What if I sang a wrong note?

But I shouldn't have spoken to Jay like that. Oh my god. I just told him to shut up! I want to turn around and say that I'm sorry. But the word won't come out of my mouth.

"Fine. Be like that," Jay says.

Beck puts in earbuds to listen to music. I fold my arms and sit in uncomfortable silence.

Then Beck pulls out an earbud. "Listen to this! Bombargo just dropped a new single!"

He passes me the earbud, and I put it in. Wow, this tune is amazing. Upbeat and fun. With depth. "Play it again," I say as it finishes.

"Sure!"

"Can I hear it?" Jay asks. He's talking to Beck, not to me.

"Sure!" Beck is so easygoing.

I find myself listening to one earbud while Jay listens to the other.

Jay says, "These guys really are great."

"You know them too?" Beck asks Jay.

"They're my favorite. And Pia's. Both of us love them."

For a moment it feels like it used to between Jay and me. But then I remember what he just said about me not saying sorry. I turn to him. "Could you just butt out of our conversation?"

He looks hurt but just nods. "Sure, Pia."

For some reason this makes me more mad. The whole awful day piles up on me. Of course, it doesn't actually pile up on me, but it feels like it does. I feel like I'm underneath the weight of every single horrible thing that's happened today.

"It's your fault we fought, Jay. Don't pretend otherwise." This comes out of my mouth very loudly. Everyone on the bus turns toward us.

"Whatever, Pia."

"You keep expecting me to be different. Better. Maybe I can't be any better! Ever thought of that?" I ask. My voice is loud, like Pippa's.

"Settle down, Pia," says Miss Singhal.

"You don't need to be the best all the time, Pia," says Jay.

"Just stop talking to me. I never want to speak to you again," I say. Still loud.

Jay stares at me. I can see the hurt in his eyes.

"Fine," he says.

Miss Singhal seems as surprised as everyone else on the bus. "Pia, that's enough. One more word out of you, and you'll be in trouble."

More trouble.

Chapter Nine

We arrive at the meet. As soon as we're off the bus, Jay storms away. Panda B. sticks out her tongue at me. Miss Singhal goes over to the registration table. She gets out numbers and hands them out. I'm going to tell her my ankle hurts too much for me to race.

But I can't admit it. And part of me keeps hoping my ankle will somehow be fine.

It's the most confusing feeling. And thinking about it makes my heart race. I check my pulse. No one around notices me. I watch other people passing by. Some are laughing. The field is large, and over on one side there's a high jump happening. People are cheering. I watch a girl leap over an impossibly high bar. Wow. She must feel amazing. She must have just beaten a record.

I notice a giant rabbit coming across the field.

Of course, it's not really a giant rabbit. It's a kid wearing a rabbit costume. It's our school mascot. But there's something different about the rabbit mascot today.

There's something about the rabbit that I recognize.

Something about how it moves.

As it gets closer, I see its eyes in the cut-out eye holes.

It's Jay! He's dressed as the school mascot! That's why he was on the bus. He looks completely ridiculous in the rabbit costume.

"What are you doing?" I ask as he goes past.

"I thought we weren't speaking."

"Right," I say. "Well, we're not. But I want to know why you volunteered to be the school mascot today."

"To watch you race."

"Why?"

"I know how important winning is to you."

There is a long, awkward pause. I feel like he's waiting for me to apologize. For being so angry about my surprise birthday. For being so horrible to him on the bus. But I just can't. Anyway he was mean to me too. He told Beck I never say sorry!

Jay hops forward on two feet. "See you later. Good luck with your race."

"Um, thanks," I say. I spot Mom and Nia coming over to me. "Nia!" I cry. I give her a big hug. "How are you doing?"

She smiles. "I think we caught my migraine early enough. The medication helped."

"That's awesome, little sis. I'm so happy you noticed the signs."

"Well, you noticed."

"Yeah but this time you did what you needed so it wouldn't get worse."

"I actually feel totally fine right now. It makes me want to learn how to manage my migraines better."

"Do you want me to install that app?" I have an app on my phone that tracks migraines. Mom has the same app on hers. But Nia has always refused to install it.

She looks straight into my eyes. Sometimes we can do the freaky twin thing. I know what she's going to say before she says it. "Yes," she replies. "Thanks."

I feel a little shift inside me. I feel a tiny bit of worry disappear. If Nia learns to manage her migraines, I might not have to worry about her so much.

"Why today?" I ask suddenly.

"What do you mean?"

"Why did you decide to take your meds right away today?"

She smiles at me. "It was because of you. Don't laugh at me, but you were so brave with your ankle.

You took charge. You took control. And you looked after me! Even though you were hurt. I want to be able to do that too."

The announcer calls for the 400. "I have to go race," I say.

She can read me, just like I can read her. She grips my shoulder. "Your ankle hurts, Pia."

I stare at her. "But I have to win this race."

"Why?"

I don't hesitate. "I'm the best at 400 meters. I need to be the best at this. And at school. And everything."

I notice something in her gaze. She seems sad.

That's when I realize something. If *I'm* always the best, then Nia must always be *second* best.

Miss Singhal calls me over. "Come on, Pia! You've got this in the bag."

"You're always the best to me," Nia says.

"Thanks," I say. I am about to say that back to her, but she interrupts.

"Please don't hurt your ankle more."

"I think it's okay," I lie.

"You're lying."

I shake off her grip. "I have to go." I walk toward the starting line, refusing to show my limp.

After this race I have some thinking to do. This awful day has made me look at stuff differently. Maybe.

But I don't have time to think about any of that now.

I look over at Jay. Jay the giant rabbit.

I remember that I wanted to win this race to prove to him how wrong he was. Do I still feel like that? I don't have time to think about it.

I stand at the start. I am as ready as I'll ever be.

The start gun goes off. I take one step—on my good leg.

Then I step onto my other leg.

And my ankle buckles.

I can't race.

I actually can't do it.

I pause. The other runners are already streaking ahead.

I turn to look at my sister. Her eyebrows are furrowed. Mom is standing beside her, eyebrows furrowed. They look the same.

Next to them, Jay is watching me too. He really does look ridiculous dressed as a giant rabbit.

But it gives me a great idea.

Rabbits hop.

With two feet.

Humans hop.

With one foot.

I have one good ankle. I can hop!

I lift my bad leg.

I take one hop forward.

On my good leg.

And then another hop.

The other runners are far ahead. Panda B. is in the lead.

I hop again.

And again.

I hear cheering. Panda B. has won.

I still have a long way to go. My good leg already feels tired.

I hop.

Hop.

Hop.

I look over at Mom. She has her hand over her mouth. This is what she does when she's worried.

I see Nia and Jay glance at each other. Jay the rabbit. I see that there's a fuzzy carrot on the front of his costume. I've never noticed it on the mascot before. It strikes me as very funny.

Suddenly the words strive for balance pop into my head. They strike me as funny too. Because I am hopping on one leg, I am not balanced at all. I giggle. And hop.

I look at my sister and my friend. "I could do with a little help over here!" I yell.

It's all they need. They both run over to me. They each take one of my arms to hold me up.

Together they help me hop, hop, hop.

The crowd is quiet, watching, even though the race is over. Then one kid starts cheering. "Go, team!"

Soon everyone is cheering and yelling. "Go, team! Go, team! Go, team!"

The sound makes me feel like I have wings.

Of course, I don't really have wings. I have a sore ankle. But I feel like I'm flying.

Chapter Ten

At the end of the race I hug Nia first. "Thank you, little sister."

She puts a finger quickly to my lips. "Maybe you should stop saying that." She takes her finger away.

"Saying what?" I ask.

"Little sister."

"But you *are* my little sister."

She shakes her head. "No. I'm really not."

I sigh. "I guess you're right. I should stop thinking of you like that."

"You're not responsible for me. We look out for each other."

Mom arrives at the finish line just in time to hear this. "Your sister's right, Pia. You're not responsible for her," she says. "I am. And so is your father. Nia, monkey, come with me. I think your sister has someone she needs to talk to first. We'll wait for you over by the stands, bear."

Mom smiles at me. I haven't talked to her about what happened with Jay and me, but somehow she seems to know. I can tell from the way she's looking at me. I feel like maybe I could trust Mom next time I have a problem. Maybe later I should tell her about some of the feelings I've been having.

As Nia and Mom walk away, I turn to Jay. The words I should have said ages ago have become unstuck from deep inside me. Suddenly it seems very easy to say what I need to say.

"I'm sorry."

He grins. "That's okay. I shouldn't have thrown a party for you. I knew you wanted to study."

"I aced the test in the end. I'd already studied. I should have been grateful for the party. It was the first time in my whole life that someone has thrown a party just for me. A party I didn't have to share with Nia. I'm just so sorry for wrecking it all. Will you forgive me?"

He looks at me through the eye holes in the rabbit costume. "Pia, we're friends. It's all good. We're good."

"Even though I was so mean to you on the bus? I'm sorry for that too."

"Okay. You can stop apologizing now! You never need to apologize again." He laughs. "I was mean on the bus too. I'm sorry about that."

I look at him. I reach out to touch the fuzzy carrot on the mascot's belly. "I've never noticed this before."

"I put it there. I sewed it on. I thought it was funny."

"It's ridiculous!"

He grins. "I thought you'd notice it. You're so good at noticing things. You notice what people need, and you're so thoughtful. I miss having you in my life."

Just then Beck walks over to us. "You two still arguing?" I can tell by his grin that he's joking.

I glance at Jay. "No. We're over it."

"Good. Because that was so awkward on the bus. And also good because I have something I want to ask you both," Beck adds.

"What?" I am very curious.

"I'm doing tryouts for my band. I need to replace the guys who left, remember?"

I nod. My heart rate is going up. I move my fingers to my wrist to check.

"For your *band*?" Jay says.

"Yeah. I was asking around, and apparently you're pretty good on the drums, Jay."

Jay shrugs. I can tell, even through his rabbit costume, that he's pleased.

"And Pia," Beck says, "you said you've been writing some song lyrics. And you sing. Right?"

I nod. Now my heart is racing. I don't have time to join a band. I have to study. And do better at track—I can't lose another race. And what if I'm not good enough for the band? What if I fail?

But even though my heart is racing, it's also saying something. Of course, my heart is not actually talking to me. But it feels like it is. It feels like it's saying, *Write songs! Try out for the band.*

What if I fail?

But what if I don't?

I remember how I felt writing the poetry earlier today. What if I got to write songs and I felt like that all the time? Calm and happy?

"Right. So, yeah. I will try out for your band," I say. "Thank you. And yes you can interview me too. Even though I didn't win the race, I have a lot to say!"

My heart speeds up so fast it feels like it might race out of my chest. But nothing happens. My heart stays in my body. Of course it does. And then it slows down again and beats at normal speed. It's weird. Because I feel okay.

Mom calls out, "Pia, are you coming? It's time to go home."

I'm about to walk over to her when I remember.

I'm not going home. I still have detention.

I freeze.

What's Mom going to say? I have detention. I want to join a band. She's going to think I'm going off the rails! She's going to think I'm delinquent!

I can't tell her. Not about detention. Not about wanting to join the band.

"What's wrong?" Jay asks.

I whisper, "I have detention."

Beck drops his voice to a low whisper. "I do too. Why are we whispering?"

I gasp. "You're a bad kid! First band. Now detention. I can't be friends with you!"

Beck and Jay burst out laughing.

"I'm not a bad kid," Beck says. "I just have trouble getting to class on time. I get distracted. I got detention for being late for the fifth time in a row."

"Oh." He's right. It doesn't sound that bad.

"Is that how everything is for you?" Beck asks. "Everyone has a label? Good kid, bad kid, smart kid, happy kid? What are you? A perfect kid?"

"I—" I'm about to answer, but my mom has walked over.

She says, "Yes, she's a perfect kid." She smiles. "Come on, honey. Let's go home."

I stand to face her. On my wobbly ankle.

"I'm not perfect," I say. And then I start to cry.

Chapter Eleven

Mom and I sit on the grass at the side of the field. I'm glad not to have weight on my ankle. Nia, Jay and Beck are waiting out of earshot. They keep sending nervous glances over at me.

Mom says, "What's going on, Pia?"

"I've had the worst day. Ever," I say. "I lost the race. I messed up my math test. I have…"

"Hey, hey, that doesn't sound so bad," she says.

"I have detention."

She looks at me with surprise. "Really?"

"I'm really, really sorry, Mom. And I want to join a band."

She holds both hands up. "Whoa! Pia! One thing at a time. What's the detention for?"

"I accidentally caused a food fight." I dip my head down into my hands. My tears are flowing freely now.

To my shock, Mom laughs. "You won't believe this, but I caused a food fight when I was at school too. I was so mad at my friend that I threw a meatball at her!"

"Really?"

"Really. Pia, we all make mistakes."

"I actually didn't cause the food fight. I just fell over. And then the broccoli..."

"Your ankle," Mom says, pointing at my leg. "You need to think about how you dealt with that today."

"I know."

"You should never have walked on it. Let alone raced. You should have called your dad or me right after you fell. You could have been seriously hurt."

"I know. I'm sorry. But I didn't want to lose."

"And I admire that about you, Pia. But the fact that you push yourself to be the best isn't the best thing about you."

"It isn't?"

"No. You are a kind, tender and fantastic person, Pia. But really, you're you. And I love you for that. Nothing else."

"Even though I got detention?"

"Yes. I'm not happy that you have detention. But I know that you'll go. And then it will be over. It's not the end of the world."

"I guess not."

I see Dad's car pull up. "Did I miss the race?" he calls out, running toward us.

"Dad is always chaos. And you're always so

perfect," I say quietly. "I thought I was like you, but today I was more like him."

"I'm not perfect, bear. No one is. And anyway, you may be a bit like both of us. But most of all, you're like yourself," Mom says. She smiles at Dad.

Since the divorce it's always a bit awkward between them. But it is getting less awkward every time.

"I missed it, didn't I?" Dad says. "I'm so sorry, Pia."

"That's okay. Mom and Nia were here. And Jay. Anyway, I didn't win."

"I still would have liked to watch."

"That's okay, Dad. Could you give me a ride back to school? I have detention." I swallow, but I don't look down.

He gives a quick bark of laughter. "Really?"

"Really. It's not funny."

"No, ahem. Of course not." He glances over at Mom. Even she seems amused. "Well, you'll have to tell me all about it in the car. C'mon."

"Thanks," Mom says to Dad. "I'll take Nia home."

"I'll ask Beck if he wants to come with us," I say to them.

"Beck?" asks Mom.

"He's the guy in the band I want to join."

"Right. About that," Mom says. "Do you think you have time for another activity? You've seemed very stressed recently."

"I have been stressed," I say. "And I think joining a band would actually make me less stressed. Writing songs makes me feel calm." Even saying the words fills me with happiness. "And happy," I add.

"Why don't we talk about it some more later?" Dad looks at my mom. "Maybe we can have a family meeting. But for now, we need to get you back for this detention, you little troublemaker." He is smiling at me as he says it.

I wave Beck over, and we head toward the car. I look back at the field. Panda B. is smiling. Her mom is taking photos of her. I realize that for her, today was a great day.

And for me? Well, it wasn't the day I thought it would be. It wasn't a great day. But as I wave goodbye to Jay and Nia and get in the car with my new friend, I realize it wasn't such a bad day after all.

And who knows what tomorrow will bring?

My mind plays with that sentence, and with the idea of good days and bad days. The idea of good kids and bad kids. The idea of perfect. I pull out my phone. Beck leans over and asks what I'm doing.

"Writing a song. Well, a first draft. I can always rewrite it later." I smile at him.

"Awesome," he says.

And I realize that it *is* awesome. It absolutely is. I say, "I think I might call the song 'All My Plans.'"

"Cool," he says. "Can't wait to hear it."

I get back to writing, letting the calm and happy feeling take me over.

Acknowledgments

Thank you to my editor, Tanya, and to the Orca team for these great books. And thank you to everyone at WCA, including Pia!

Ava's life goes sideways
when she inherits an
African gray parrot.

Chapter One

Ava sits on her white sheets. She leans over to fluff her blue pillows. She snaps a selfie. Then deletes it. *Yuck!* She pouts. Snap. Delete. Pout. Snap. *Perfect!* She draws squiggles and hearts around herself in the photo. She types some text on top:

> **Good morning! Beautiful day. Time for breakfast with the fam. Lucky me!**
>
> **#homelife #perfect #Sundays**

She posts it to her 542 followers. No! Now there are 543. Excellent! Her post isn't really true. There won't be any family breakfast today. There's never any time for that. Not since Dad left. This morning Mom is busy working in her home office. And Ava's stupid brother, Gregg, is still asleep.

Ava's phone flashes. She has two likes already. So what if her post isn't true? People *like* it. A couple more little hearts appear. Both of her BFFs post comments.

@journey314 You are soooo pretty Ava girl!!!

@purevision Breakfast with your hot brother.

#swoon #luckyforsure #perfectfamily

Ava imagines herself as a famous online celebrity. She flies all over the world. She gets tons of free stuff. She goes to all the best parties and galas.

Ava is still daydreaming about her fantasy life when her mom comes into her room. She is wearing a gray suit, and her hair is freshly cut and colored. But her eyes are red. She has been crying.

"Honey, I have something to tell you," her mom says, not looking at Ava. She rearranges the one book that is out of place on Ava's white shelf.

"What's wrong?"

Ava's mom sighs. She pushes her hair back, and some of it sticks straight up. Ava notices that one of the buttons on her mom's suit is missing. Which is weird because even though she works at home, Ava's mom likes to look perfect. Right now she looks like a hot mess.

"This came in the mail on Friday. I didn't open it because I've been very busy." Her mom holds out an envelope with a handwritten address on it. "I actually thought it was a charity asking for money. I didn't think..." She wipes her eyes. "Oh, just read it, would you?"

Ava takes the envelope and pulls out a letter. The paper is very thin. It has loopy handwriting on it. There are a few blotches.

Dear Ava,

I remember when you came to visit. You were seven. And so cute! You loved Mervin so much. It is my dying wish that you look after him well.

With all my love,
Great-Uncle Bertie

Her mom's phone buzzes. She checks it, sighs and glances at Ava. "I guess it's true. I just got a message from the lawyer. Great-Uncle Bertie is dead."

"Great-Uncle Bertie is dead?" Ava reads the words again. "Wait a minute. Who is Great-Uncle Bertie?"

"Nana's brother. You only met him once. He was very busy sailing all over the world. Huge traveler. No wife or kids. We met him in a hotel in London when we went to Europe. Remember, he had a room in that fancy hotel? That's where he lived when he wasn't at sea."

"I don't remember him at all."

"Well, he clearly remembers you!"

"What does he mean when he writes 'you loved Mervin so much'? Who is Mervin?"

"The lawyer says that Mervin is a parrot."

"A parrot?" Ava's face screws up. "Oh my god! I do remember. That old gray bird. Super grouchy, from what I remember. Surely that thing can't still be alive."

"Parrots live for years, Ava." Two tears fall down her mom's cheeks.

"I'm sorry, Mom. You must miss Uncle Bertie so much."

"No, that's not it. I hardly knew the old man. You don't understand. His parrot is coming to live with us. In our house."

"There's no way!"

"Listen, if you hadn't been so friendly with that bird, none of this would have happened. We can't have a parrot here."

She's totally right. A parrot would not look good on Ava's online profiles. She has a spotless, white room. The accent color is light blue. The feature image on the main wall is an anchor—Ava loves the sea. Well, she loves the *idea* of the sea. Living in a big city, she doesn't actually get to the ocean that much.

"We can say no, right?" Ava asks. "I don't know anything about parrots. I can't look after a parrot."

"I don't see how we can, honey." Her mom's eyes narrow. "It was Great-Uncle Bertie's dying wish." Her eyes become even more narrow, until they close. This is the face she pulls when she wants to shut out the world. She releases a slow breath. Ava knows she is counting to ten.

"I guess you're right, Mom."

"Great-Uncle Bertie is probably laughing in his grave."

Ava frowns. "Why?"

"He always said I was too obsessed with being neat and tidy. Too obsessed with image. Now he's putting a filthy bird in my house." She opens her eyes.

"There's nothing wrong with wanting a clean house. Or a good image."

Ava's mom smiles. "You are a girl after my own heart. We'll figure out how to stop that parrot from coming here. Dying wish or not. I'll message the lawyer." She taps on her phone.

Her phone buzzes in reply. She reads the screen, then holds it up for Ava to see.

Mervin already on his way. Express Post. Should arrive this afternoon. He's an African gray parrot. With a nasty bite!

"I'm not looking after a parrot, Mom!" Ava yells. "You have to stop this!"

There's a thud in the next room. It's Ava's big brother jumping out of bed. He appears at her doorway, scratching his chest. He's tall, with dark hair and eyes.

Her BFFs think he's hot. Over the last year he has gone from being a skinny, annoying boy into the guy they all want to get to know. Ava can't understand what they see in him. Right now he's in worn-out sweats that are stained with coffee. He farts.

"Get out!" Ava yells.

"Not until I find out what's going on in here," Gregg says. He always has such a loud voice.

"Quality family time," says Ava sarcastically.

Their mom closes her eyes and breathes out.

"Seriously, what's all the yelling about?" Gregg asks. Even more loudly.

Ava holds out the letter. Gregg snatches it. He reads it and then collapses into laughter. "You're getting a parrot, Ava? Miss Prissy Pants?"

"What? Are you five years old? Don't call me that."

"We should put it right here. On your empty desk that looks so perfect because you never use it!" He falls onto Ava's bed, laughing harder.

Their mom squeezes her eyes more tightly shut.

"See?" Ava says to no one. "A perfect family Sunday."

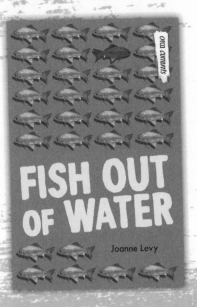

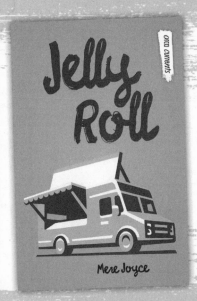

Jenny is looking forward to her March Break retreat. Until she finds out that the boy who bullies her at school is going too.

Xander and his friends get in over their heads during a role-playing game in a supposedly abandoned hospital.

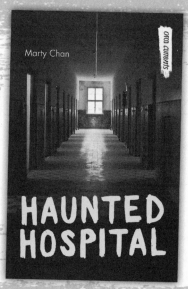

Alice Kuipers has written many books for young people, and they have been published in dozens of countries. Her work has also been made into plays and produced for radio. She lives with her family in Saskatoon, Saskatchewan.

For more information on all the books
in the Orca Currents line, please visit
orcabook.com.